PIE Is for SHARING

Stephanie Parsley Ledyard

Illustrated by Jason Chin

A NEAL PORTER BOOK
ROARING BROOK PRESS
NEW YORK

For Megan —S.P.L.

For Noah, Chloe, Eka, and Keya —J.C.

Text copyright © 2018 Stephanie Parsley Ledyard

Illustrations copyright © 2018 Jason Chin

A Neal Porter Book

Published by Roaring Brook Press

Roaring Brook Press is a division of Holtzbrinck Publishing Holdings Limited Partnership

175 Fifth Avenue, New York, NY 10010

The artwork for this book was created using watercolor and gouache.

mackids.com

Library of Congress Control Number: 2017957298

ISBN 978-1-62672-562-1

Our books may be purchased in bulk for promotional, educational, or business use. Please contact your local bookseller or the Macmillan Corporate and Premium Sales Department at (800) 221-7945 ext. 5442 or by e-mail at MacmillanSpecialMarkets@macmillan.com.

First edition, 2018

Printed in China by Toppan Leefung Printing Ltd., Dongguan City, Guangdong Province

3   5   7   9   10   8   6   4

Pie is for sharing.

It starts out whole
and round.
Then . . .

you can slice it
into as many pieces
as you wish.

Almost.

A book is for sharing.

A ball is nice for sharing, too.

And a tree?

A tree is always shared . . .

even when you think it is yours
alone.

Other things for sharing:

a jump rope,

your place in the middle,

a rhyme,

time,

a boat,
a stream,

your towel, warmed by the sun.

Easy to share:

cousins,
sticks,

stones from your pocket.

Hard to share:
your best friend.

If you are hurt,

it helps to share a hug,

and some bandages,

and the story about what happened.

Hideouts and treasures,
these are good to share.

Words and music are made for sharing.

So are berries
and the last piece of homemade bread.

Even the crumbs.

Many can share one light.

And a blanket?
A breeze?
The sky?

These are for sharing.

Just like pie.

OCT   2019

21982319269183